3-Minute Stories

Best-Loved Tales

 publications international, ltd.

CONTENTS

The North Wind 4

Androcles and the Lion 12

Stone Soup 20

Smart Manka 28

The Boy Who Cried Wolf 36

The Tailor's Apprentices 44

The Ant and the Grasshopper 52

What a Good Man Does 60

The Magic Doll 68

The City Mouse and the Country Mouse 76

Paradise 84

The Selfish Giant 92

Rikki-Tikki-Tavi 100

Prince Carrots 108

The Nightingale 116

The Bell of Justice 124

The Seal Skin 130

Icarus and Daedalus 140

Ali Baba 150

The North Wind

Adapted by Lisa Harkrader
Illustrated by Beth Foster Wiggins

Nate's mother handed him a leather money pouch. "Go to the village," she said. "Buy oats for our dinner."

Nate ran to the village and bought a basket of oats. The North Wind began to blow. He blew until the oats were gone.

"I must find the North Wind," Nate said.

Nate walked through the night to the North Wind's house.

"What is it?" the North Wind asked.

"I bought oats," said Nate. "You blew them away."

"It is my job to blow the wind," said the North Wind. "But you were brave to come here. I'll give you this, instead."

The North Wind handed Nate a tablecloth.

"Tell it, 'Cloth! Cloth! Serve food!' You will never be hungry again," the North Wind said.

Nate stopped at an inn for dinner. He spread the cloth on the dinner table.

"Cloth! Cloth! Serve food!" Nate said.

A roast beef sprang from the cloth. Up popped potatoes, carrots, bread, and cake. Nate ate and ate. The innkeeper stood in the doorway. He gave Nate the very best room.

"Mother, look!" Nate said the next morning. "Cloth! Cloth! Serve food!"

His mother watched. The cloth did not do anything.

"I think you have been tricked," his mother said.

Nate walked through the cold to see the North Wind.

"What is it now?" the North Wind asked.

Nate told him that the tablecloth did not work.

"This isn't the cloth I gave you," said the North Wind. "This one is torn. But you were brave to come here."

The North Wind handed Nate a piggy bank.

"Say to it, 'Bank! Bank! Make money!' You will never be poor again," the North Wind said.

Nate stopped at the same inn.

"Bank! Bank! Make money," Nate said.

Coins dropped from the bank. Nate handed the coins to the innkeeper. The innkeeper gave Nate the very best room.

The next morning, Nate ran all the way home.

"Mother, look!" he said. "Bank! Bank! Make money."

His mother watched. The piggy bank did not do anything.

"I think you have been tricked," his mother said.

Nate set out to find the North Wind.

"You again!" said the North Wind. "What is it this time?"

Nate handed the piggy bank to the North Wind.

"It doesn't work," Nate said. "You tricked me again."

"I blow the wind," said the North Wind. "I don't have time for tricks. This is not the same bank. This bank is chipped."

"The innkeeper!" Nate said. "The innkeeper has tricked me."

"I have something that you can use against tricksters," the North Wind said, handing Nate a rope. "Tell it, 'Rope! Rope! Tie him up!' You will never be tricked again."

Nate set off for the inn with the magic rope.

"What have you brought tonight?" the innkeeper asked.

"Only this magic rope," said Nate.

Nate was given the very best room. In the middle of the night, the innkeeper slipped into the room. Nate sprang from his bed. "Rope! Rope! Tie him up!" Nate said.

The rope slithered around the innkeeper's legs. It wrapped around his arms. The innkeeper could not move.

"Give back the tablecloth and the bank," Nate said.

The innkeeper told Nate where the tablecloth and the bank were. Then Nate untied the innkeeper.

Nate ran all the way home. He spread the tablecloth on the table. He put the piggy bank on the cloth.

"Mother! Look!" Nate said. "Cloth! Cloth! Serve food! Bank! Bank! Make money!"

It was amazing! A pot of stew sprang up from the cloth and coins spilled from the bank.

Nate and his mother never went to bed hungry again.

Androcles and the Lion

Adapted by Sarah Toast
Illustrated by Yuri Salzman

In ancient Rome there lived a poor slave named Androcles. His cruel master made him work from daybreak until long past nightfall. Androcles had very little time to rest and very little to eat. One day, he decided to run away from his harsh master, even though he would be breaking the law.

In the dark of night, Androcles got up from the miserable heap of straw and rags that served as his bed. Crouching low so he was no taller than the bushes that dotted the fields, the young slave moved swiftly away from his master's land.

Clouds covered the moon that night, and Androcles crossed the open fields unseen. It was only when he came to the wild woods that Androcles dared to stand up tall again.

Androcles found a sheltered place at the foot of a tall tree. There he lay down on a bed of pine needles and fell fast asleep.

When Androcles awoke, he hiked deeper into the woods so he wouldn't be found by his master. He looked for water and something to eat. But other than a few berries, there was no food.

Day after day, Androcles searched for food. And day after day, he went hungry. Androcles grew so weary and weak that at last he was afraid he wouldn't live through the night. He had just enough strength to creep up to the mouth of a cave that he had passed many times. Androcles crawled into the cave and fell into a deep sleep.

As Androcles lay sleeping, a lion was hunting in the woods nearby. The lion liked to sleep in the daytime and hunt for his food at night. The lion set off for his cave as the morning began to fill the sky with light.

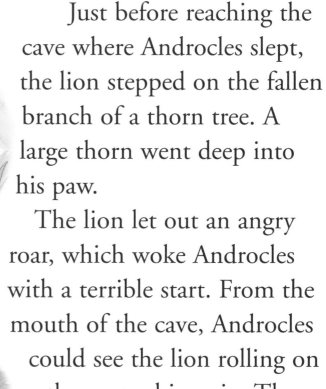

Just before reaching the cave where Androcles slept, the lion stepped on the fallen branch of a thorn tree. A large thorn went deep into his paw.

The lion let out an angry roar, which woke Androcles with a terrible start. From the mouth of the cave, Androcles could see the lion rolling on the ground in pain. The lion's roars echoed loudly in the cave.

Androcles was terrified that the lion would attack him. But the lion held out his hurt paw to Androcles. Even from a distance, Androcles could see the large thorn in the lion's paw.

Androcles found some courage and came closer. He slowly sat down on the ground near the beast. To Androcles' astonishment, the huge lion flopped his great paw into the young man's lap.

Androcles spoke soothing words to the lion as he carefully pulled the thorn from the lion's paw. "Don't worry, handsome lion. We'll have this thorn out in no time," he said softly.

When the thorn was gone, the lion rubbed his head against Androcles' shoulder and purred a rumbling purr. The lion was grateful to Androcles and didn't even mind that Androcles had moved into his cave.

The lion slept most of the day. And at night, he hunted for food while Androcles slept. Each morning, the lion would bring meat to Androcles, who'd build a fire to cook his meal.

One morning, as Androcles was cooking what the lion had brought him, five soldiers suddenly appeared.

"We saw the smoke from your fire," they said. "We have come to arrest you for running away from your master."

Androcles tried to run from the soldiers, but they were too fast for him. Three soldiers sprinted after Androcles. When they caught him, they tied his hands behind his back.

The lion awoke with a start. Before he could get to his feet, the other two soldiers threw a strong rope net over him. They attached two ends of the net to a stout pole and carried the angry lion out of the woods.

Androcles was locked in one cell, and the lion was locked in another. As was the custom in Rome at the time, the man and the lion would battle. Hundreds of people gathered to watch.

Androcles heard a trumpet blast. The bars to his cell were opened. Androcles was pushed onto the field. The trumpet sounded again, and the bars to the lion's cage were opened.

The lion crouched only for a moment, but in that moment he recognized his friend from the forest. The lion bounded across the arena in three long leaps. He stopped right in front of Androcles—and then he gently lifted his paw.

The crowd of people in the arena was stunned.

"How did you tame this ferocious lion?" the emperor asked.

"I merely helped him when he needed help, Your Highness," Androcles replied. "That is why he spared my life."

The emperor freed Androcles and the lion. The lion returned to the wild woods, and Androcles became a free man in Rome. Androcles often went for a walk in the woods to visit his good friend, who never forgot him.

Stone Soup

Adapted by Jennifer Boudart
Illustrated by Kevin O'Malley

A traveling man walked along a dirt road. He had a feather in his hat and a smile on his face. His name was Jack Grand, and he was a rat-a-tat man. A rat-a-tat man could do all sorts of things. He could tumble, dance, walk on his hands, yodel, hum, drum, sing, whistle, and whittle. He even knew some riddles.

Despite the fact that he could do many things, sometimes he was hungry.

"There must be something to eat around here," he said.

Jack Grand continued down the road until he reached a small town. He knocked on the first door he found.

Jack stepped back behind the stone gate.

"May I help you?" asked a young woman.

"Hello," he said. "I'm Jack Grand. I can tumble. I can dance. I can walk on my hands. I'll do a few tricks to pay for a meal."

"I am sorry," said the woman. "I have no money for a rat-a-tat man. And I only have a pinch of salt and a pinch of pepper. Try next door."

Jack hurried to the next house. He knocked on the door. A man answered. Jack swooped his hat from his head. "May I help you?" asked the man.

"Hello," he said. "I'm Jack Grand. I can yodel. I can hum. I can play the drum. I'll do a few tricks to pay for a meal."

"I'm sorry," said the man. "I have no money for a rat-a-tat man. I have only a head of garlic. Ask next door."

Jack did. He knocked on every door in the village. He swooped his hat from his head. He bowed low to the ground. Nobody had enough food to share.

One woman had only potatoes. Her neighbor had only a few carrots. One family had only some bacon. Another family had only a handful of beans.

Jack sighed and set off down the road. He walked along for a while. He no longer had a smile on his face. He decided to sit down and rest. He saw a stone. This stone was not like the other stones in the road. The stone gave Jack an idea.

Jack knocked on the first door in the village.

"I know you have no food to share," Jack said. "But do you have a big pot I could borrow?"

"A big pot?" asked the woman.

"I'm going to make stone soup," Jack said.

"Stone soup?" she asked.

Jack nodded.

In a moment, the woman returned with a big pot.

Jack carried the big pot to the village square. He filled it with water, and carefully lit a fire underneath. When the water was boiling, Jack dropped the stone into the pot.

The pot bubbled and brewed. Jack tasted the soup.

"Is it good?" asked the woman.

"Yes," said Jack. "Actually, it is very good. It would only be better with a little salt and pepper. Not much. Just a little."

"Salt and pepper?" she asked. "I have salt and pepper."

The woman ran to her cottage as fast as she could. She returned with a salt shaker and a pepper mill.

Jack sprinkled the salt and pepper into the pot. He stirred. The pot bubbled and brewed. Jack tasted the soup.

The man next door came out of his cottage.

"Is it good?" asked the man.

"Yes, it's good," said Jack. "It would only be better with a little garlic. Not much. Just a little."

"Garlic?" the man asked. "I have garlic."

The man ran home and returned with a head of garlic.

By this time, the entire village had gathered around Jack.

"It's actually good," Jack said. "It would only be better if…"

"If what?" asked the villagers.

"Potatoes," said Jack.

A woman ran to get potatoes.

"A bit of bacon, some carrots," said Jack, "and some beans."

The villagers ran to get the food. Jack threw it all into the pot and stirred. Jack tasted the soup.

"Is it good?" everyone asked at once.

"Yes," said Jack, "and it's done."

Everyone ate until the pot was empty. Empty, that is, except for the white stone.

Jack tumbled, danced, walked on his hands, yodeled, hummed, played a drum, sang, whistled, and whittled. He even told some riddles. When he was done, he waved to the villagers.

Jack walked for a while. He saw a rock. It was shiny and black. He picked it up and put it in his pocket.

"It's actually perfect," Jack said, "for making rock stew."

Smart Manka

Adapted by Jamie Elder
Illustrated by Pat Hoggan

Manka was a smart woman. Her father was upset about a cow that a farmer was supposed to give him for his hard work. But the farmer kept the cow.

"Father, we must go to the judge," Manka said. "The judge is a very fair man. He will be able to help us."

They went to see the judge and explained the situation.

"To be fair, we must ask the farmer to come discuss this," the judge said.

The judge listened to the men as they told their stories.

"This man deserves payment," the judge said. He ordered the farmer to give the cow to Manka's father.

After the matter of the cow, Manka and the judge began to spend a lot of time together. They were both fair and smart.

"Manka," the judge said, "I would like you to be my wife."

"I would like you to be my husband," Manka said.

"There is just one thing," the judge said. "People know you are smart. They will think you can change my mind about my decisions. You must promise not to interfere."

"I promise not to interfere," Manka said.

"If you should, I will ask you to leave my house," said the judge. "It would not be right. People would talk."

"You are also smart and fair," she said. "I won't interfere."

Manka and the judge were married that very spring.

One day, a man who Manka did not know greeted her.

"Good day, Madame," he said. "Is your husband home?"

"No, he isn't," she said. "I could give him your message."

"Ask him to change his mind about my colt," the man said.

"What is the matter with your colt?" Manka asked.

"It just doesn't belong to me anymore," he said. "My mare gave birth to a colt under a wagon. The wagon owner said the colt belonged to him. The judge agreed with him."

"That doesn't sound right," Manka said.

"I didn't think so either," the man said. "I couldn't argue with the judge, though. He is usually fair."

"I think I can help you," she said.

Manka knew she was interfering, but she also knew that her husband had made a bad decision. She invited the man in and told him of her plan to help him get his colt back.

As planned, the man came back the next day. He cast his fishing rod into the dusty road. When the judge saw him, he was puzzled. He got up from his meal and went outside.

"Sir," the judge said. "May I ask what you are doing?"

"Of course," the man said. "I am fishing."

"You cannot catch fish in a dusty road," the judge said.

"It is possible," the man said.

"How is it possible?" the judge asked.

"If a wagon can have a colt, a road can have fish," he said.

The judge was quiet. The man reeled in his line and waited. He hoped the judge's wife was right.

"I see your point," the judge said. "The colt is yours."

The judge went into the house. He sat across from his wife.

"You interfered," he said. "Think of how people will talk."

"They would have talked about your bad decision," she said. "I broke my promise, and it's only fair that I go. I was trying to be a good wife to you. I was also trying to be a fair woman."

"You are a fair woman," the judge said. "And you are a good wife even today. Take the one thing you like most from our house. Maybe it will remind you of me."

Manka and the judge ate dinner together one last time. The judge drank a little too much wine and feel asleep. Manka loaded him into the horse cart and drove to her father's house.

"Where am I?" the judge asked in the morning.

"You said that I should take one thing from the house," Manka said. "I took what I liked the most. You."

The judge looked at Manka for a long time. He smiled.

"Oh, Manka," the judge said. "Please, come back home."

"Of course," Manka smiled. "It is the fair thing to do."

The Boy Who Cried Wolf

Adapted by Jennifer Boudart
Illustrated by Jon Goodell

There was a young boy who lived in a village. He was not very old, but he had an important job to do. He was a shepherd, and his job was to guard the sheep from danger, especially from wolves in the forest.

The shepherd boy also had to make sure the sheep got plenty of food and exercise. Every day, in order to give the sheep the exercise they needed, the boy took them to a nearby valley. Once they had walked there, the sheep would graze on the tasty green grass that grew in the valley. The villagers trusted the shepherd to take good care of the sheep. The villagers were nearby. If a wolf ever did attack, the people could run to the rescue.

Every day, the shepherd faithfully watched the sheep. For the shepherd boy, every day was the same. The sheep looked the same every day. The forest looked the same, too. Some days he wished that something exciting would happen.

In his whole life, the boy had never seen a wolf come near the sheep. In fact, he had never even seen a wolf! The boy never even heard any howling.

"This is not any fun at all," thought the shepherd boy. "Would it be so bad to pretend there was a wolf?"

As the sheep ate the grass, the boy cupped his hand near his mouth and shouted, "Wolf! Wolf! A wolf is stealing the sheep! Come help me!"

All the village people stopped what they were doing and ran to help scare off the wolf. When they got there, they were very confused.

The villagers did not find a wolf. And where was the shepherd? They were worried about him. What if the wolf had stolen the boy? Frantically, they searched high and low.

A villager pointed to a tree and said, "There he is!"

They saw he was not hurt. In fact, he was laughing!

"You looked so funny running up here for no reason," laughed the boy.

The villagers did not laugh. They shook their heads and said, "We have to get back to work. We don't have time for pranks."

The shepherd boy did not hear a word they said. He was laughing too hard.

The next day, the shepherd boy's mother and father told him to be good. He nodded his head and left.

Soon, however, the boy was bored again.

"Wolf! Wolf!" he shouted, louder than the day before. "A wolf is stealing the sheep! Come help me!"

The villagers came running. And again, all they found was a silly little boy.

The villagers were very upset. They shook their heads and told the boy, "If you don't tell people the truth all the time, they will never know when to believe you."

The boy was still laughing at his joke. After the villagers went back to their jobs, however, he started to think about what the people had said.

"Maybe," he thought, "it isn't so funny to play tricks on others." The boy began walking back to his lookout post.

Little did he know he was soon going to have all the excitement he could handle.

Just on the other side of the trees, a sly wolf had seen everything. When the shepherd boy reached his post, the wolf began stealing the sheep. The shepherd boy could not believe it.

It was a real wolf! He cried out, "Wolf! Wolf! A wolf is stealing the sheep! Come help me!"

The boy waited for the villagers to come running, but no one came. They were not going to fall for that trick again!

The boy tried yelling for help, but no one came. He watched as the wolf ran into the forest with all the sheep.

The shepherd boy ran into the village. "Wolf! Wolf!" he cried. "He's stealing our sheep!" The boy kept running and calling for help, but no one believed he was telling the truth.

Finally the shepherd boy stopped running. The boy knew no one would believe him. How could he blame them? When they trusted him, he let them down. He lost their trust.

The young shepherd walked back to his lookout post and gazed down where he always took his sheep to eat grass. But there were not any sheep left.

The wolf had taken all of them away.

The shepherd boy was so sad, he began to cry. He learned, the hard way, that there was nothing funny about lying.

The Tailor's Apprentices

Written by Leslie Lindecker
Illustrated by Mike Jaroszko

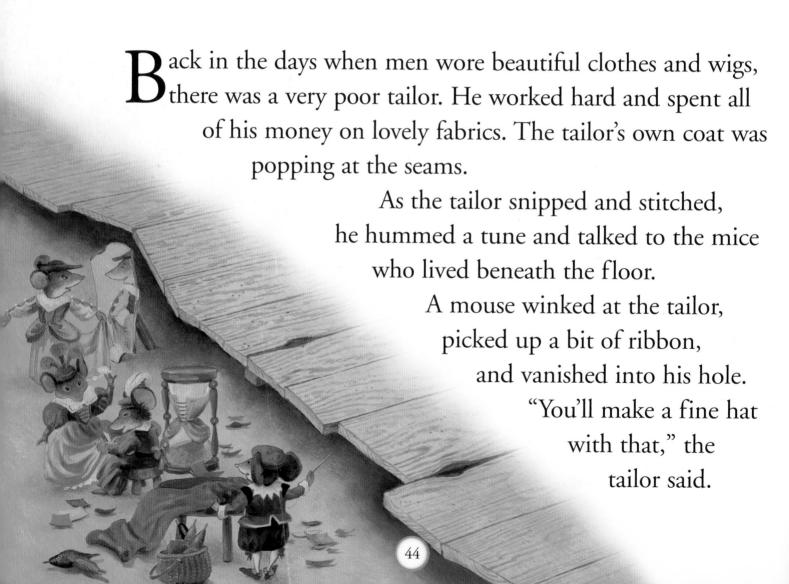

Back in the days when men wore beautiful clothes and wigs, there was a very poor tailor. He worked hard and spent all of his money on lovely fabrics. The tailor's own coat was popping at the seams.

As the tailor snipped and stitched, he hummed a tune and talked to the mice who lived beneath the floor.

A mouse winked at the tailor, picked up a bit of ribbon, and vanished into his hole. "You'll make a fine hat with that," the tailor said.

"My little friends," the tailor continued, "soon you shall have the finest bits of lace and thread, because I am going to make the mayor's suit for his wedding!"

The tailor measured and marked, and measured again. He cut out the coat from the emerald cloth. "No wasting fabric," the tailor said. "Just enough for a suit for a mouse, and such a grand suit, all stitched with gold!"

Soon, the table was covered with cut pieces. There were buttons and bows, flaps for the pockets, and cuffs for the sleeves. The floor was littered with bits of green and gold thread and lace. Everything was ready to begin sewing the beautiful emerald suit, except for one spool of thread.

The tailor heaved a sigh, took off his spectacles, and rubbed his eyes. "We will begin again in the morning, my friends. I am tired."

The tailor pulled on his old, worn-out coat, snuffed the candle, and stepped out of his shop into the snowy night. He fastened the window latch and locked the door, putting the key into his pocket. The tailor shuffled through the snow and up the rickety stairs to the room he rented above his shop. The tailor lived alone with his cat, whom he called Tomkin. As he unlocked the door, Tomkin meowed. "Tomkin, old friend," said the tailor, "fortune has finally smiled upon us, but I am worn out beyond working this night."

The tailor built up the fire in the grate, then called to his cat. "Tomkin, old friend," the tailor said, "I need you to go to the shopkeeper. I must have a spool of golden thread for the mayor's new suit. Please don't forget."

The tailor tied his last dollar to Tomkin's collar, then opened the door for the cat. Tomkin walked slowly into the cold night. Although he was usually a faithful cat, Tomkin wasn't fond of the cold. Besides, Tomkin had mice on his mind.

Tomkin spent much of his time chasing the mice. They were often too fast for him. But that day, Tomkin was especially lucky. He had caught many mice that morning. Saving them for his supper, Tomkin trapped the mice under bowls and cups. After his walk in the cold, he would enjoy a fine meal.

The tailor was very tired. "I fear I have a touch of the flu," he said as he felt his forehead. He went to bed and talked to himself about the mayor's beautiful suit.

Suddenly, the tailor heard a tip-tip-tap coming from somewhere in the small room. It was the faintest of tip-tip-taps, and he was weak with fever, but still he went to investigate. The tailor searched under the bed. He searched under the sink. He looked under the rug. He looked under the table. He could see nothing, but he continued to hear the tip-tip-tapping.

At the sink, his teacups and mugs, bowls and pots were all turned upside down. From under one of the teacups he heard the tip-tip-tap again.

Slowly the tailor lifted the teacup, and out popped a lovely lady mouse. She smiled, wiggled her long brown nose at him, and scampered away.

The tailor took off his spectacles and rubbed his eyes. Then he heard a scritch-scritch-scratch. He looked under a bowl and was met with the gaze of a handsome gentleman mouse, who bowed to the tailor before running away.

"I truly must be ill, for I swear that mouse was wearing a hat!" said the tailor.

The tailor began
to turn over all the teacups and
mugs, bowls and pots to find many
little mice hopping and running about.

The tailor continued to talk to himself as he
prepared for bed. "What shall I do without that spool of
golden thread? The mayor's suit should be my finest creation!"

The little mice listened to the tailor as he muttered on about
the suit for the mayor.

Tomkin walked in with a gust of cold air. Tomkin spied the
overturned teacups and upturned bowls. He swatted a cup to
the floor in search of the fat little mice he was saving for dinner.

"Tomkin, old friend," the tailor said from his bed. "It is late
and I'm not well. Did you get my spool of golden thread?"

Being in an ill-tempered mood, Tomkin hid the spool of thread under the teapot lid. He jumped up onto the tailor's bed and kneaded the quilt with his claws.

The tailor remained in bed for several days, tossing and turning with fever. The mayor's wedding was fast approaching, and the tailor was too ill to work. No one thought at all of the tailor's tiny shop and the emerald suit that lay upon the table.

Tomkin prowled around in search of mice. He heard noises coming from the tailor's shop downstairs. Tomkin went down the rickety steps and into the snow to investigate the noise.

From the window, Tomkin could see his little brown mice, the very same ones the tailor had let go, singing and dancing — and sewing! The mice were stitching the emerald coat.

Near dawn, Tomkin heard the mice cry in chorus, "No more thread!"

Tomkin jumped down from the ledge and went up to the tailor's tiny room. The cat fetched the golden thread from the teapot and placed it upon the tailor's quilt.

The tailor hurried down the steps to the shop. Not one mouse was to be seen. But there on the table, where the tailor left the pieces of satin and silk, was the loveliest emerald wedding suit anyone had ever seen!

Everything was finished except for one buttonhole. There was a scrap of paper pinned to the buttonhole. It read, *NO MORE GOLDEN THREAD,* in tiny writing.

The tailor danced about the shop, then finished the buttonhole with the thread Tomkin had bought.

Thus began the long and good fortune of the tailor, who grew quite rich, and Tomkin, who grew quite fat.

The Ant and the Grasshopper

Adapted by Catherine McCafferty
Illustrated by Jason Wolff

Summer had just begun. "Summer's here! The best time of the year!" the grasshopper sang. "Warm sun, lots of fun!"

A line of ants marched past the grasshopper, carrying small seeds and bits of food. As they walked along, some crumbs fell to the ground. Before the ants could get them, the grasshopper had eaten the crumbs.

The biggest ant walked up to the grasshopper. "We've worked very hard to gather this food," said the ant. "You should have helped us pick up what we dropped."

"That's what's wrong with your summer song," the grasshopper sang. Then he said, "You're always working. Summertime is for play, not work."

"Summertime is for planning and gathering," said the ant. "It's time for getting all the food we will need for the winter."

"Winter is so far away, I think I'd rather play," said the grasshopper hopping away.

"Wait! What about the food you took?" the ant asked.

"Oh, yes. Thank you." The grasshopper pointed toward a field. "And over there is a whole field of wheat to replace your crumbs. I like cornfields better myself, but that might be too far for you to walk." And the grasshopper hopped off.

The grasshopper leaped onto a cornstalk. A soft leaf gave him a bed. Above him, another leaf gave him shade. "Those ants can gather and work and store. I'll just snooze right here and snore." He fell fast asleep.

Meanwhile, the ant lined his home with seeds and other foods. "When the snow is on the ground, we will be nice and warm in our nest. We will have plenty of food to eat and plenty of time to play," thought the ant.

All that summer, the grasshopper watched the ants. When he saw them going to a picnic for crumbs, he hopped along to eat his fill. While they carried food back to their nest, he slept in his cornstalk bed.

Then one day, the grasshopper heard a loud noise. The farmer was coming to harvest the corn! Down came the leaves and the corn the grasshopper had feasted on all summer.

"Close call, all in all," sang the grasshopper. "Did you see that?" he asked the ant as the line of ants marched past. "I just lost my bed and food! Isn't that so very rude?"

"The days are getting shorter, my friend. But there is still time for you to store food and find shelter," the ant answered.

"Not today, I've got to play," the grasshopper sang.

All throughout the fields and forests, he saw squirrels gathering nuts and ants gathering crumbs.

The grasshopper frowned. The grasshopper shivered. He looked around for a sunny spot, but the sun was already gone from the sky.

The ground seemed colder, too. One day, the grasshopper tried to nibble an apple. He found that it was frozen. "I don't like my apple in ice," said the grasshopper. He was so chilly that it was hard to think of a second line to his rhyme.

The ground was so cold that it hurt his tiny feet. "Where are those ants, now that I need them?" sang the grasshopper. Suddenly snow began to fall. It covered the grasshopper.

He had to get inside or he would freeze! Hopping as fast as he could, the grasshopper raced to the ant's home. "Anybody home?" he called as he stepped into the tunnels.

"Why aren't you out playing in the snow?" asked the ant.

The grasshopper wanted to say that he had just come by for a visit. But he could feel the cold wind on his back. Sadly, the grasshopper sang, "I should have listened to what you said. Now I'm cold and scared and unfed."

The ant understood. But he wanted to be sure that the grasshopper understood, too. "We got our food for the winter by working hard," he said. "If you stay with us this winter, you'll have to work hard, too. Your job here will be to sing for us. Every day." Then the ant laughed. "Because winter is our time to play."

All that winter, the grasshopper sang for the ant and his family. And the next summer, the grasshopper sang a song as he helped to gather food. "Summer work is slow and steady. But when winter comes, I'll be ready!"

What a Good Man Does

Adapted by Lisa Harkrader
Illustrated by Debbie Pinkney Davis

Mr. and Mrs. Goodley had been married for forty happy years. They were happy because they always agreed.

Mr. and Mrs. Goodley had a neighbor. His name was Chauncey. Chauncey could not believe they always agreed.

"You can't agree about everything," said Chauncey.

"Why would we disagree?" asked Mrs. Goodley. "My husband is a good man. What a good man does is always right."

"And my wife is a good woman," said Mr. Goodley. "What a good woman does is always right."

Chauncey knew there was something that would make them disagree. Mr. and Mrs. Goodley had two prizewinning cows. Chauncey decided to talk to Mrs. Goodley about them.

"Why do you need two cows?" Chauncey asked her. "You and Mr. Goodley don't drink much milk. One cow is plenty."

Chauncey knew Mr. Goodley would never part with his cows. Mr. Goodley talked to the cows like they were people.

"You're right," said Mrs. Goodley. "It's time to sell a cow."

"Sell a cow?" said Mr. Goodley. "Our cows are prizewinners. They've never been apart. You want me to sell one of them?"

Mrs. Goodley nodded. Mr. Goodley was quiet for a moment. Chauncey smiled. He was certain they would finally disagree.

"How sensible!" said Mr. Goodley. "It's the most sensible thing I've ever heard! We don't need two cows when one will do. And the one cow will soon have a calf."

"Then we will have two cows again!" said Mrs. Goodley.

Chauncey could not believe it. Mr. Goodley, who loved his cows so much, took one of the cows to town. Chauncey went with him. On the way to town, they met a man with a horse.

"This man might want your cow," Chauncey said. "Perhaps he would be interested in trading his horse for your cow."

"That's a brilliant idea!" said Mr. Goodley.
He traded his cow for the horse.
Chauncey smiled.

"You started with a cow," he said. "Now, you have a horse. Your wife will be surprised."

"Yes, she will," said Mr. Goodley. "We need a horse to pull our cart. It's sensible. My wife will agree."

Chauncey almost believed it, but he was not ready to give up just yet. Soon, they met a man with a pig, which gave Chauncy a good idea.

"This man might want your horse," suggested Chauncey. "You could trade it for his pig."

Mr. Goodley agreed. He traded his horse for the pig.

"You started with a prize cow," Chauncey said. "Now, you have a loud, squealing pig. Your wife will be surprised."

"Yes, she will," said Mr. Goodley. "She'll think it's smart."

Chauncey almost believed it, but he was not ready to give up. Soon, they met a man with a goat. Chauncy suggested that Mr. Goodley trade his pig for the goat. Mr. Goodley traded his pig for the goat. He traded his goat for a goose. He traded his goose for a duck. And he traded his duck for a rooster.

"You have ended up with a skinny rooster," Chauncey said.

"The rooster will crow each morning when the sun rises," said Mr. Goodley. "We'll never sleep too late again!"

Mr. Goodley and Chauncey were very hungry. They passed an inn. Mr. Goodley looked at Chauncey.

"You could trade the rooster for food," Chauncey said.

"Splendid idea!" said Mr. Goodley.

Mr. Goodley and Chauncey ate until their bellies were full. The two men walked home. Mr. Goodley had nothing left.

"Your wife won't like this," Chauncey said. He suddenly felt bad for starting the whole thing.

"Oh, yes she will," said Mr. Goodley.

"I'll bet you a hundred dollars that she will be furious," Chauncey said.

"I'll take that bet," said Mr. Goodley. "She won't be furious. I'll win that bet."

When the two men finally reached home, Mrs. Goodley was waiting for them.

"I traded our cow for a horse," said Mr. Goodley. "It was a fine horse."

"A horse! How sensible!" said Mrs. Goodley.

"Yes," said Mr. Goodley, "but I traded the horse for a pig. I then traded the pig for a goat. I traded the goat for a goose. I traded the goose for a duck. I traded the duck for a rooster."

"Finally, all that trading made us hungry," he continued. "I traded the rooster to the innkeeper for our supper."

"For your supper?" asked Mrs. Goodley.

Chauncey did not smile this time. He felt bad.

"How clever!" she said.

Chauncey shook his head. He gave up. He handed Mr. Goodley a hundred dollars.

"We couldn't have gotten a hundred dollars for our cow," said Mrs. Goodley. "My husband is a good man."

"And what a good man does is always right," Chauncey said.

"I'm glad that we all can agree," said Mr. Goodley.

Magic Doll

Adapted by Jamie Elder
Illustrated by Nan Brooks

Russia is a far and distant land. Long ago, a beautiful girl lived there with her family. Her name was Vasilissa.

Vasilissa was still very young when her mother became ill. She was sick for a very long time. One night, she called to Vasilissa. Vasilissa went to her and stood by her bed.

"My beautiful daughter," said her mother, "we will not be together for much longer. I am very sick."

Vasilissa saw that her mother was holding a little doll.

"I have kept this doll for you," her mother said. "She will protect you. She will help you when you are afraid. Feed her a bit of food. Then whisper your thoughts to her. She will tell you the right thing to do. Keep her with you always. Remember that I love you. I will be watching over you."

Vasilissa took the doll. She kissed her mother.

Her mother closed her eyes.

Vasilissa knew she was gone.

Vasilissa was very afraid. She took the doll out of her pocket and fed her some bread and milk. Then she whispered her thoughts into the doll's ear.

"Vasilissa," the doll said, "you must not be afraid. Close your eyes and rest. Things will be a little better in the morning."

In the morning, Vasilissa woke up. She did not feel so afraid. She was still sad, but she knew the doll protected her. She also knew her mother was watching over her.

Vasilissa grew up to be a beautiful young woman. She took good care of her father. He was very proud of her. Vasilissa knew her father was lonely.

"Papa," she said, "you must marry again. I know you loved my mother, but you are lonely. You do not need to be lonely."

"I am not lonely when you are near," he said.

Time passed. Vasilissa's father met a woman. She had a daughter of her own. Vasilissa hoped they'd become a family.

The woman was cold and mean. She married Vasilissa's father only because he was a rich merchant. Her daughter was cold and mean, too.

They made Vasilissa do all the hard work. They made fun of her while she did it. Sometimes, they even laughed at her.

Vasilissa was afraid of them.

That night, she fed her magic doll some bread and milk. Then she whispered her thoughts into the doll's ear.

"Vasilissa," she said, "do not be afraid. Close your eyes and rest. Things will be better in the morning."

In the morning, Vasilissa woke up. She didn't feel afraid. She knew hard work always paid off. She knew the doll protected her. She also knew her mother was watching over her.

Vasilissa's father was often away. She missed him very much. He had to work hard. He had to make money to take care of his family.

Vasilissa's father did not know how poorly Vasilissa was being treated. She did not want to upset him. She knew he worked hard.

Vasilissa did not know the stepmother had a plan. She sent Vasilissa to fetch water. She did not want Vasilissa in the cottage. She wanted to talk to her daughter alone.

"We must be rid of Vasilissa," said the stepmother. "Now that stepfather is away, we will send her to Baba Yaga's house."

It was nighttime when Vasilissa returned with the water. She found that the cottage was dark inside.

"We have no light," said the daughter.

"Go to Baba Yaga's house for a candle," said the stepmother.

Vasilissa went to look for Baba Yaga's house. It was said to be deep in the forest. It was said that no one ever returned from it. Vasilissa walked for a long time. She saw a light in the trees. She knew it was Baba Yaga's house when she got closer. It had to be! An old woman peeked out of the window.

"What do you want?" she asked.

"Only a candle," Vasilissa said.

"There is a price to pay even for a candle," Baba Yaga said.

Baba Yaga opened the door to her house. Vasilissa stepped inside. She was surprised by all the strange things she saw. Baba Yaga had many pets. She even had snakes. She also had strange things on her shelves. There were bones on the floor!

"It's too late for candles," Baba Yaga said. "It's time for sleeping. We'll discuss the candles in the morning."

Vasilissa did not know what to do. She did not want to end up like the bones on the floor. She held her magic doll close to her. She did not have any bread or milk to feed her.

She tried to remember what her magic doll always told her. Her doll always told her not to be afraid. Her doll told her to close her eyes and rest. Her doll told her things would be better in the morning.

Vasilissa lay down on the floor. She trusted her doll.

In the morning, Baba Yaga woke Vasilissa. She gave Vasilissa a list of chores to finish before she returned.

Vasilissa nodded. She knew she had to work fast.

Soon, Vasilissa was finished, and Baba Yaga returned from her walk in the forest.

"Did you finish everything on the list?" Baba Yaga asked.

"Yes," Vasilissa said. "I finished everything. I promise."

"How did you do it?" Baba Yaga asked.

"I am blessed," Vasilissa said. "My mother is watching over me."
"One who is blessed cannot be here," Baba Yaga said. "Go!"

Vasilissa ran. She ran until she reached the cottage. The stepmother and her daughter were gone. But her father was there!

"My beautiful daughter," he said. "I have missed you."

Things were always better in the morning. Hard work did pay off. The magic doll did protect her.

Her mother was watching over her, too.

The City Mouse and the Country Mouse

Adapted by Michelle Rhodes
Illustrated by Kathleen McCord

In the heart of the country there lived a little mouse. He loved the sound of squirrels chattering. He liked to listen to crickets chirping. Country Mouse loved the smell of dirt and grass. Country Mouse never wanted to live anywhere else.

In the city lived his cousin. This mouse loved the sound of cars honking. He liked to watch people. City Mouse never wanted to live anywhere else.

One day, Country Mouse
invited City Mouse to visit him.
Country Mouse spent all morning
cleaning his little house. Then he sat by the
entrance to his hole and waited for his
cousin to arrive. He listened to the birds
singing. "I can't wait to see my cousin,"
Country Mouse said.

At the same time, City Mouse
left his city apartment and traveled
toward the country. There were no
tall buildings in the country. But City
Mouse was excited to see his cousin.

When City Mouse arrived, he set his fine leather suitcase at the door and asked, "Is this hole your basement, cousin?"

"No, silly," said Country Mouse, "this is my house." Country Mouse brewed some dandelion tea for his cousin, and they settled into their oak leaf beds for the night.

The next morning, City Mouse woke up to the sound of chirping birds. "What is making all that terrible noise?" asked City Mouse.

"That is the sound of morning in the country," said Country Mouse. "Now come help me. We have a busy day ahead of us." City Mouse followed Country Mouse as he raked pine needles and gathered acorns.

In the afternoon, City Mouse sat near the old oak tree and wiped the sweat from his brow.

"You work too hard, cousin," said City Mouse.

The next day, City Mouse asked Country Mouse to come with him to the city.

Country Mouse agreed to take a vacation to the city to see where City Mouse lived. When they arrived at the hotel where City Mouse lived, they crawled inside the building through a small crack in the wall. "This is my apartment," said City Mouse.

Country Mouse saw fancy napkins, golden candlesticks, and fine china. "We are under the bandstand," said City Mouse. "At night, the band plays and people dance until early in the morning."

"How can you sleep with all that loud noise?" asked Country Mouse.

"I usually sleep during the day," said City Mouse. "Now, I believe, it is time to find dinner."

The mice went to the kitchen where the chef was rushing back and forth from the pantry. As soon as the chef left, the mice scurried into the pantry.

After they nibbled their fill, City Mouse said, "Now it is time for dessert."

City Mouse led Country Mouse into the dining room where people were busy eating their dinners.

The mice tiptoed to a pastry cart filled with delicious cakes. Country Mouse was about to taste a cream puff when the cart lurched forward. Country Mouse toppled into the chocolate cake!

At the cart's next stop, the mice got off and found themselves back in the kitchen. Just then, the chef saw the mice. "You pesky mice," he said. "I'll get you!" The chef chased after the mice with a broom, but City Mouse led Country Mouse safely through another crack in the wall.

Country Mouse fell on the ground to catch his breath. "That was too close, cousin," he said. "I'm going back to the country where it's safe."

Country Mouse gathered all his things and walked back home to the peaceful country. As he neared his favorite oak tree, Country Mouse heard the crickets chirping and said, "It's good to be home."

Back in the bustling city, the band played and City Mouse said, "It's good to be home."

Paradise

Adapted by Lisa Harkrader
Illustrated by Amy Flynn

Tom and Lucy lived on a farm, but they did not have much. They had a plow, a tractor, and an old hen named Madge. The name of their farm was Paradise.

"It doesn't feel like paradise," Tom always said.

Tom was very busy. He could not plow, plant, and pick the corn by himself.

Lucy tried to plow, but the plow got stuck. She tried to plant, but most of the seeds blew away. She tried to pick the corn, but she pulled too hard. All the corn was ruined, and they did not have enough money to buy more seed.

"We'll have to sell Madge," Tom said.

"Brawk!" Madge squawked.

"I'll take her to the bird farm down the road," said Lucy.

Lucy set off down the road with Madge under her arm.
Lucy walked and walked. Madge cackled and squawked.

Madge fluttered from Lucy's arms and flapped across the barnyard. Lucy ran after her.

Madge flapped through a puddle. Lucy fell in the puddle. Madge flapped through the goose pen. Lucy, in turn, slid through the goose pen. Geese honked at her.

Madge flapped through the duck pen. Lucy skidded through, too! Ducks quacked at her.

Madge flapped through the turkey pen, and fluttered through the chicken pen. Then Madge flew through the peacock pen.

Lucy followed. Mud, eggs, and feathers landed on top of her.

Madge flapped and flapped.

"BRAWWWK!" cried Madge as she ran toward Paradise.
Tom heard Madge squawk. He looked up.

A strange creature was following Madge. The creature was as big as a person. It had goose feathers on its head, duck feathers on its arms, turkey feathers on its belly, and chicken feathers on its back. Trailing behind it were the lovely tail feathers of a peacock.

Tom had never seen such a sight!

"I couldn't sell Madge," the creature said. "I may not have gotten the corn seed, but just look at all the lovely feathers I brought back."

"Lucy? Is that you?" Tom asked.

Lucy nodded.

"We had a little accident at the bird farm," Lucy said. "I don't think Madge wants to be sold."

"Well, I'll sell her," Tom said.

Tom set off down the road with Madge under his arm. Tom walked and walked. Madge cackled and squawked.

They came upon a house. A woman was standing in the yard. She held a cup in one hand. She raised the cup over her head and counted to ten.

"Full!" she said.

The woman slapped her hand over the cup and ran inside.

"Oh no!" Tom heard the woman cry. "Not again!"

"Howdy, ma'am," he said. "My name is Tom. I live down the road at a place called Paradise. Do you want to buy a hen?"

"Brawk!" Madge cried.

"I don't need a hen," said the woman. "All I need is sun. Sunshine flows into the cup when I stand outside. I put my hand over the cup so it won't escape. Then I run inside. But…"

"You lift your hand," Tom said, "and the sunshine is gone."

"Yes," the woman said. "How did you know? Oh, I would happily give five hundred dollars to the person who could bring sunshine into my house."

"I can help you," Tom said.

Tom picked up an ax and chopped a hole in her wall.

"Now you have a window," he said, "and sunshine."

"I always wanted a window," the woman said. "I was afraid it would be too much work. Thank you!"

The woman handed Tom five hundred dollars.

Tom tried to give it back, but the woman insisted.

When Tom and Madge reached Paradise, Tom could not believe his eyes. The fields were plowed, and they were planted in feathers!

"Well?" Lucy asked. "What do you think?"

A breeze blew across the farm. Goose and duck feathers fluttered. Turkey feathers fluttered. Chicken feathers fluttered. Peacock feathers fluttered, too.

Tom smiled. He had a wonderful wife, money in his pocket, and even his old hen.

"What do I think?" he asked. "I think our farm is paradise."

"Brawk!" Madge agreed.

The Selfish Giant

Adapted by Lisa Harkrader
Illustrated by Tammie Lyon

Jacob raced to catch up with Matthew and Rachel. They were leading Jacob to the castle on the hill. The castle towered above them. It was big and had many windows. It was also empty. The windows were dark, and the doors were bolted shut. The owner had been away for years. He had been away for so long nobody remembered him.

The garden surrounding the castle was wonderful. Birds twittered in the trees. Butterflies flitted from flower to flower.

Jacob, Matthew, and Rachel tossed their jackets and books in the grass. Matthew and Rachel ran through the garden, playing tag. Jacob did not want to play tag. He saw a tree in the corner of the garden. Hanging from each branch were ripe peaches. Jacob ran to the tree. He stretched to reach a peach.

"What are you doing?" a booming voice asked.

Jacob turned around. An enormous man was standing inside the gate. He was a giant! His legs were like tree trunks. His feet were like boats. His chest was like a barrel. He was so tall his head brushed the tallest branches. He was so big the ground shook when he walked.

"Get out of my garden!" the giant yelled.

Matthew and Rachel scrambled through the grass. They grabbed their jackets and books. They ran past the giant. They went through the gate and ran from the garden.

Jacob just stared at the giant.

"Your garden?" Jacob asked. "Nobody lives here."

"I live here," the giant roared. "I went away, and now I'm back. This is my garden. I don't need wild children ruining it."

"We're not ruining anything," Jacob said. "We're not wild. It's so wonderful here. We were just playing."

"It's mine!" yelled the giant. "Get out!"

"You're just, you're just…selfish!" Jacob said.

Jacob, Matthew, and Rachel stayed far away from the castle for a long time. Autumn turned to winter, and winter turned to spring. Jacob and his friends played in the park.

"It's not like playing in the castle garden," Jacob said.

"Maybe the giant will go away again," Matthew said.

"We should go look," Rachel said.

Jacob and his friends ran to the castle.

They could no longer see the garden. The giant had built a stone wall around it. On the wall was a sign. It read:

KEEP OUT!

ESPECIALLY CHILDREN

"Let's look over the wall," Jacob said.

A pile of firewood was stacked against the wall. They climbed the stack and peeked over the wall.

Snow covered the grass. A cold wind whistled. The trees were bare.

Outside the garden, the days were becoming warmer. The sun was brighter. Flowers blossomed. Butterflies danced.

Inside the garden, it was still winter. The trees were not budding. There were no birds.

"It is no longer wonderful," a voice cried. "It's always winter."

It was the giant. He was leaning over a rosebush. The giant reached down to touch its only rose, but its petals crumbled and fell.

The giant sighed and shook his head. He looked sad.

Matthew and Rachel climbed down from the firewood. Jacob felt so sad. He turned to climb down, lost his balance, and one of the stones from the wall came loose. Matthew and Rachel helped him move the stone. They wiggled it until the stone finally broke free. The hole went through to the garden.

Jacob climbed into the hole and crawled through to the other side. Suddenly it was spring in the garden! Jacob ran to the peach tree. He stretched to reach a peach.

"You'll never get it like that," said a booming voice.

A huge hand picked him up from the ground. Jacob turned.

"Thank you," Jacob whispered to the selfish giant.

"No," said the giant. "Thank you. You were right. Children don't ruin gardens. They fill them with spring."

The children went to the garden every day after that. They became great friends with the giant. They taught the giant to play tag. The giant lifted them up to pick peaches.

Together, they chased butterflies all spring.

Rikki-Tikki-Tavi

Adapted by Brian Conway
Illustrated by Richard Bernal

This is the story of a brave little mongoose named Rikki-Tikki-Tavi. One day, a big flood rushed through the jungle. It swept Rikki-Tikki-Tavi out of his hole.

Rikki-Tikki-Tavi was brave, but he could not fight the flood. When it was over, he had been washed away. He was far from his home. Everything hurt. Even the tip of his tail hurt. He could barely move, but he heard some friendly voices nearby.

"Is it a cat?" asked Teddy, a young boy.

"It's a mongoose," said Teddy's mother.

The boy picked Rikki-Tikki-Tavi up from the mud and carried him home. Soon, Rikki-Tikki-Tavi started to feel better. He looked around. His new friends seemed very kind.

"Can I keep him?" Teddy asked.

"He is a wild animal," his mother said. "He will go wherever he wants to go."

Rikki-Tikki-Tavi ducked under a towel for a nap.

"It looks like this is where he wants to be," Teddy laughed.

Rikki-Tikki-Tavi liked Teddy's house. Teddy was always willing to play. But Rikki-Tikki-Tavi still wanted to do the things a wild mongoose did. In the garden he made many new animal friends. His best friend was Darzee. She was a beautiful songbird.

One day, when Rikki-Tikki-Tavi and Darzee were playing, Rikki-Tikki-Tavi heard a low hiss behind him. He knew that there were two snakes living in the garden, Nag and his wife Nagaina. They both had angry, red eyes.

"My family has ruled this garden for thousands of years," Nag said. "Every animal here must fear me."

"I am not afraid of anything," Rikki-Tikki-Tavi said. "I may be a small mongoose, but I am brave."

That night, while the family slept, Rikki-Tikki-Tavi stayed awake. He heard the sound of snakes moving along the rug. Rikki-Tikki-Tavi went toward the bathroom. The snakes were whispering in the dark. Rikki-Tikki-Tavi crept closer until he could hear what they were saying.

Nag and Nagaina were making evil plans.

"We must scare the big ones away," Nag whispered. "Then there will be no one to help the little mongoose."

"The garden will be ours again," Nagaina said. "Our eggs will hatch and our children will rule this entire garden."

"Our family will rule for a thousand more years," Nag said.

Rikki-Tikki-Tavi watched Nag move away. Quietly, he crept up behind him. He heard a loud sound. Nag's body went limp. Rikki-Tikki-Tavi saw Teddy's father standing over them. He had a broomstick. He had hit Nag over the head with it.

Teddy's father dropped the broom and picked up the brave mongoose. Rikki-Tikki-Tavi knew he'd have to fight Nagaina. She would want revenge.

Rikki-Tikki-Tavi found Darzee and told her his plan.

"While I go take Nagaina's eggs," he said, "you must help keep her busy."

Darzee hopped toward the house.

Nagaina saw Darzee. She began to slither toward her, but then stopped. Nagaina found something more interesting.

"Hurry, Rikki-Tikki-Tavi!" Darzee shouted. "Nagaina is on the porch. She has Teddy cornered!"

Rikki-Tikki-Tavi ran as fast as he could to the house. He rushed up to the porch and dropped an egg beside Nagaina.

"I have hidden the rest of your eggs," he said.

"What have you done with my babies?" hissed Nagaina as she snapped at Rikki-Tikki-Tavi, who quickly leapt away from her fangs. Nagaina's tail hit her egg, and it rolled off the porch. She grabbed it in her mouth and hurried to bring her egg to safety.

Nagaina slid into her hole. Rikki-Tikki-Tavi leapt for her tail. He grabbed it, and Nagaina dragged him down with her. Nagaina dropped her egg again, and Rikki-Tikki-Tavi grabbed it.

"I will not harm your family," Rikki-Tikki-Tavi said bravely. "You must promise not to harm mine. I put your eggs in the meadow beside the river. Get them and never ever return."

Nagaina took her egg and left the garden forever.

Teddy and his parents had saved Rikki-Tikki-Tavi after the flood. Rikki-Tikki-Tavi had returned their kindness.

Rikki-Tikki-Tavi lived with Teddy and his family for a long time. His nights were spent under Teddy's warm covers. His days were spent playing in the garden with Darzee.

The garden was his own little jungle kingdom.

Prince Carrots

Adapted by Jamie Elder
Illustrated by Kathy Mitchell

There once was a time when there were many kings and queens. Their children were princes and princesses.

One of these princes was Prince Carrots. He was not very handsome. In fact, he was very hard to look at. His face was too wide. His nose was too long. His mouth was too big. And his hair was so orange, he came to be called Prince Carrots.

The queen loved her son just the same.

The queen's best friend was Mercury the Magician.

"Don't worry," Mercury said. "He will be very intelligent."

"Can you make him more handsome?" the queen asked.

"No," Mercury said, "I cannot make him what he is not. But I can give him a special gift. Prince Carrots can give his intelligence to the person he loves the most."

It was true that Prince Carrots grew up to be intelligent.

"Do you know about the Trojan War?" the king asked.

"Of course, Father," Prince Carrots said. "Helen was kidnapped by a Trojan named Paris. Greek soldiers hid in a giant wooden horse that was taken to the gates of Troy. The soldiers spilled out of the horse and saved Helen."

"Where do pearls come from?" the queen asked.

"Oysters make pearls from sand," Prince Carrots said.

"How do you make a berry disappear?" Mercury asked.

"Eat it as fast as you can," the prince said.

Prince Carrots knew how to make people laugh. He knew the very best jokes. At parties, everyone gathered around him.

A princess from a nearby kingdom noticed his smile. It was so big, she could not help but notice it.

Prince Carrots saw the princess looking at him. He was surprised because she was the most beautiful princess he had ever seen. She had a perfect face. He could not look away.

Prince Carrots went to her and introduced himself.

"I am Prince Carrots," he said.

"I am Princess Pia," she said. "I am honored to meet you."

"Really?" the prince asked. "You are?"

"Yes," she said. "You are very smart. I have been told that a thousand times."

Prince Carrots sat next to her. He told her a joke, but she did not laugh. She just looked at him. Her eyes were blank. She did not understand his joke.

"Don't you like to laugh, Princess?" he asked her.

"I don't know," the princess said. "I am not very smart."

"But you are very beautiful," he said. "Are you sure you are not smart?"

"Yes," she said. "I've been told a thousand times."

"How did you get to be so beautiful?" the prince asked.

"I was born that way," the princess said.

Princess Pia told him a story. She had heard the story a thousand times. She only remembered things if she heard them a thousand times.

"My mother has a friend," the princess said. "He is a magician. When I was young, my mother worried that I was not very smart. The magician told my mother that I would be able to give my beauty to someone, a person I loved the most."

The prince nodded. Mercury had given him a similar gift.

The princess found the prince to be a good listener. He was hard to look at, but he smiled a lot. She liked that.

The prince loved the way he felt around her. He did not even feel ugly when he was with her. The princess loved the way she felt around the prince. She did not even feel stupid when she was with him.

Soon things were different between them.

"Did I tell you about the Trojan War?" the prince asked.

"Yes," she said. "Did I tell you what happened at breakfast?"

"No," the prince said.

"I told everyone about the Trojan War," the princess said.

The prince laughed! He looked wonderful when he laughed. When they were apart, they missed each other.

When he combed his hair carefully, he thought only of her. He worried, though. He told her the same things over and over. Perhaps she'd think he was stupid.

Princess Pia could not wait to see the prince. She didn't want to forget things that happened at breakfast. She didn't even bother to comb her hair. She was sure that he thought she was ugly.

"She is lovely even when her hair is tangled," he thought.

"He is smart to repeat things so I'll remember," she thought.

"Will you marry me?" the prince asked.

"Yes!" the princess said.

No one could believe it. No one, except Mercury. He knew love was like that.

It seems we become most what we want to be when we are in love. But what really happens is we are loved for what we truly are.

115

The Nightingale

Adapted by Brian Conway
Illustrated by Robin Moro

The emperor of China had the most beautiful palace. People came from all over the world to see it.

"I can show you the most beautiful thing in all of China," the head gardener told them. He led the visitors to a forest of very plain trees. He pointed at a bird on a branch.

"What is so beautiful about that?" they asked. "You led us all the way out here? You wanted us to see a plain gray bird?"

"It is no ordinary bird," the gardener said. "Just wait."

The nightingale started to sing. His voice was beautiful. The nightingale made everyone feel joy. The nightingale became known as the most beautiful creature in all of China.

The emperor of China was very old. He stayed inside. He liked his palace and his gardens, but nothing brought him joy.

One day, the emperor received a letter from Japan.

"I have heard of your nightingale," the emperor of Japan wrote. "I must see this beautiful bird. I will visit in two days."

The emperor was puzzled. He called for his head gardener.

"The emperor of Japan is coming to see my nightingale," the emperor said. "Do I have a nightingale?"

The head gardener nodded. He brought the nightingale to the emperor.

"An ordinary bird?" the emperor asked.

The nightingale began to sing. The emperor closed his eyes. He felt something he had not felt in a long time.

The emperor felt pure joy. For the first time in many, many years, the emperor was happy.

Two days later, the emperor of Japan arrived.

"This nightingale sings the most beautiful song in all of the world," the emperor of China said proudly. "Just listen."

He listened. The emperor of Japan stayed for several days. Each day he listened to the nightingale for hours. The emperor of China never grew tired of the nightingale's song either.

The nightingale's song filled the palace. It also brought visitors from all over the world.

"The nightingale sounds so lovely," the visitors said. "It's such a pity he looks so plain."

Those words upset the emperor.

He ordered a golden perch for the nightingale to sit on. He ordered jewels and ribbons for the nightingale to wear.

"Now, the nightingale will have a fine place to sit. It will look wonderful. But, it is the beautiful song that counts," the emperor of China said.

The nightingale sat on its golden perch. It wore its jewels and ribbons. It sang its song.

"Are you tired?" the emperor asked. "You must not sing if you are tired."

The nightingale continued to sing.

"You are a dear friend," the emperor said.

The emperor kept the nightingale in his private chambers at night. There were no golden perches to sit on. There were no jewels and ribbons to be worn.

"You are the most beautiful creature in all of China," said the emperor. "Jewels and ribbons make you look good, but they do not make you beautiful. You are most beautiful when you are just yourself."

The nightingale sang a special song for the emperor.

The next day a package arrived for the emperor. It was a present from the emperor of Japan.

"I hope you enjoy this gift," the card read. "It is a small token of my gratitude. The nightingale gave me great joy."

The emperor of China opened the present.

It was a small toy bird. It was brightly painted. It was covered with emeralds, sapphires, diamonds, and rubies. There was a silver key on its back. The emperor turned the key. A song played. It did not sound as lovely as the real nightingale, but it would make the emperor's visitors happy.

The emperor ordered a second golden perch. He placed the toy bird upon it.

"Now you can rest," the emperor said to the nightingale.

The visitors were thrilled.

"Finally!" they said. "A nightingale that looks as lovely as it sounds! There is nothing more beautiful in the whole world!"

But, the toy did not sound as beautiful as the nightingale.

The visitors did not seem to care that the real nightingale no longer sang. They asked for the toy to be wound over and over again. The world loved the toy nightingale.

Eventually the nightingale flew home to the forest, where he could sing for the trees and the other birds.

The emperor of China missed his friend the nightingale. He missed his beautiful song. He missed his company.

The emperor grew sick and weak. He stayed in bed.

No one could cheer him up. No one except the head gardener. He knew the nightingale could help.

"Your friend is ill," the head gardener told the nightingale. "You should go and see him."

The nightingale flew to the emperor's window. He opened his mouth. He sang a special song for the emperor.

The emperor rubbed his eyes. He sat up in bed. The color returned to his face. He was happy to see his friend again. He knew he would hear the nightingale's sweet and special songs many more times. And that is just what happened.

The Bell of Justice

Adapted by Brian Conway
Illustrated by Jon Goodell

In a little town, there hung a big bronze bell called the Bell of Justice. It was not an ordinary bell. The bell was rung only when someone needed help.

Anyone who was treated unfairly rang the bell. The townspeople were very proud of their bell because it was for everybody — rich or poor, old or young, tall or short.

One day, the mayor was walking through town when he noticed the bell's rope was terribly frayed.

"This will never do," the mayor said. "Only a tall person can ring the bell. That isn't fair. We need a new rope."

The mayor's assistant found a temporary solution. He tied a long grapevine to the bell. It hung down to the ground.

"Good," the mayor said. "There will be justice for all."

Meanwhile, a retired knight lived on a farm on the edge of town. He had owned many fine hunting dogs and many fine horses. His horses were the most beautiful in the land.

But the old knight did not hunt anymore. He sold all of his hunting dogs. He also sold all of his horses except for his favorite. The old knight's favorite horse had served him well. Now he only used the horse in festivals and holiday parades. He no longer really cared about the horse.

The old knight cared only about his money. He had a lot of it. He spent all his days and nights counting his money.

The horse did not get any attention. His coat became dirty and rough. His shoes rusted, and his hooves cracked.

The knight gave the horse a handful of hay every day. The old horse's belly ached. He needed more than hay.

The knight decided to let the horse go.

"You're a smart old horse," the knight said. "Go find your own food."

The horse wandered through the countryside.

It was a hot summer, and all the grass had dried up. All the streams had dried up, too. The horse had no food or water.

The horse followed the road to a town. Then the hungry horse spotted something wonderful. He saw a long, green vine. The vine was tied to a shiny bell. In the sunlight, the leaves were even brighter than the shiny bell.

The old, hungry horse could not resist the vine.

The horse closed his eyes, took the leaves in his mouth, and chewed and chewed. The leaves were so fresh and juicy, he could not remember the last time he had eaten anything so wonderful. The horse pulled on the vine to reach more, and the bell sounded with every pull.

The good people of the town ran to the square.

"This horse belongs to the old knight," the mayor said. "It is a noble steed."

The knight was brought to the square.

"This horse deserves justice," the mayor said thoughtfully. "Honorable knight, you have done wrong. I hereby decree that you must pay for this horse's care."

"I understand," the knight said. "I am sorry."

"Hear! Hear!" the townspeople shouted.

They built a stable for the horse. They took turns giving him food and water that the old knight paid for with his gold. The horse had plenty to eat. He was happy for the rest of his days.

"Justice has been served," the mayor said.

The Seal Skin

Adapted by Brian Conway
Illustrated by Linda Dockey Graves

Like his father before him, Sean was a fisherman. He spent his days at work on the sea. For Sean, the sea was a familiar place. He was a good fisherman.

But he was lonely.

Each night, fishermen would return from the sea and go home to their waiting families. Sean's friend, Ian, had a family.

"My wife will be happy with today's catch," Ian said. "Why don't you come for supper?"

Ian invited Sean for supper every night.

Sean always declined. Sean preferred to walk along the sea. Sean did not have a wife. He did not have a family. His cottage looked dark, cold, and empty. He was not happy.

Sean walked along the shoreline alone every night.

"The sea is a place of mystery," Sean's father used to say. Sean had heard the legends many times. He had heard stories about mermaids, magical serpents, and sea sprites. They lived in an undersea world that humans never see. Sean's father always used to take him to see the seals. His father said that some seals were regular people under their skins. They could remove their smooth skins like clothes. Sometimes, they would walk on land. Sometimes, they would even visit the village. These were the stories that all fishermen told their children. But Sean did not have any children.

He did not believe in legends, either.

As Sean walked that night, he heard high voices and cheerful laughter. Who would be out on such a cold night?

Sean walked quietly toward the sounds. He peeked slowly over the rocks. He saw three young women. The women danced on a flat rock beside the waves. They sang with clear voices. They were the most beautiful women he had ever seen.

Sean went over the slippery rocks toward them. He stepped on something. It was soft and loose. He was sure it was the smooth skin of a seal. He was very surprised.

Sean called out to them. Two of the women slipped into their skins and slid off the rocks into the tide.

The third woman saw her soft coat in Sean's hands.

"You must choose," she said. "Return my skin or dress me in clothes. If you return my skin, you will never see me again. If you give me clothes, I will be your wife."

Sean stared back into the woman's large blue eyes. They held the magic and mystery of the sea.

For the first time, Sean believed the legends.

Sean held the seal's skin close to him. He wanted to know things about the beautiful woman.

"You are a seal?" he asked.

"I am a seal when I am in the skin," she said. "When I am out of it, I am a person. I am like you."

"If you want, I will give you a wonderful life here on land," Sean said. "You will have a house in the village. You will have children. You will have everything you need."

Sean looked into her eyes. He felt love.

"But you must promise to stay forever," Sean said. "You must never return to your life in the sea."

"I promise," she said. "Take the skin and lock it away. I will wear a dress instead. I will walk on the land. I will live the life of a villager."

Sean bent down on one knee.

"Will you marry me?" he asked.

"Yes," said the beautiful woman. "I will."

Sean took her to his lonely cottage. He built a fire. She warmed herself. Sean hid the seal skin in a chest. Then he hid the key to the chest.

"I have always wanted to live among the villagers," she said. "Land is still a mystery to me. My new life with you will be an adventure."

"You will need a name," said Sean.

"I have a name," she said. "It is Mara."

The next day, Sean and Mara went to the dock. "Hello, Ian," Sean said, "I would like you to meet someone. This is Mara. She is to be my wife."

Mara loved her life on land. She loved Sean. She loved being his wife. She also loved all the people of the village. She learned their names. She learned their customs. She learned the stories they told when they gathered together.

"It is strange," she said. "The villagers tell stories about the people of the sea. My people tell stories about the people of the land."

Soon, Sean and Mara started a family. They had a daughter. They named her Sela. She had large, round eyes like her mother. She also loved the sea.

Several years passed. Mara and Sela went down to the dock every morning. They waved to Sean as he rowed to sea.

Mara watched Sean row through the waves. She looked past him. She looked out over the ocean.

She missed her people. She missed the sea.

At the end of every day, Sean rushed home. His family was always waiting for him. Sean felt like a very lucky man.

But one day, it was different. Mara's face looked so sad.

"I love you, Sean," she said. "I love Sela, too. I love you both. But I miss my people. I am sorry, Sean. I was not meant to live on land. I need to move with the tides."

Sean understood. He loved the sea, too.

"You are my family, but I do not belong here," Mara said.

Sean pulled an old, rusty key from his pocket.

"This key unlocks a chest in the shed," he said. "There you will find your seal skin."

The seal skin was neatly folded inside the chest. It was still soft and smooth. Mara clutched the skin close to her.

Sean and Sela walked with Mara. Two seals came up from the water to greet them. They called to Mara. She called back.

"I will miss you both," she said. "I will love you forever."

The two seals slid off the slippery rock. Mara slipped into her seal skin and swam after them.

Sean and Sela walked along the shore every night. Sean told his daughter many stories about the sea.

Many of the stories were legends. One story was true.

Icarus and Daedalus

Adapted by Sarah Toast
Illustrated by John Hanley

Long ago in ancient Greece there lived a very clever man named Daedalus. He was a great inventor and a skillful engineer and architect. Daedalus planned magnificent buildings. He was very proud of his skill.

Daedalus left Athens and went to the island of Crete in the Aegean Sea. He took with him his young son, Icarus.

King Minos of Crete commanded Daedalus to build a labyrinth, or maze, to imprison a fearful monster called the Minotaur. Daedalus built the maze underneath the king's palace. No one who entered could find their way out.

When the labyrinth was finished, the angry Minotaur was sealed inside. When the Minotaur was hungry, his roar shook the palace. The king was satisfied.

Daedalus had been on Crete for a long time. He was ready to return home. He went to King Minos.

"Great King," Daedalus said, "with your permission, I'd like to leave now. My work is done, and I want to return to Athens with my son."

"You know the secrets of the labyrinth," said King Minos. "How do I know you won't tell somebody how to find the way through the twisting passageways?"

"I would never do such a thing," Daedalus said.

But the king did not believe him. He ordered his guards to seize Daedalus and Icarus. The father and son were locked in a tall tower at the very edge of the palace grounds.

Daedalus and Icarus were kept under close guard in the prison tower. It would have done them no good to escape the tower, because King Minos also ruled the surrounding seas. The king's soldiers inspected every ship that left Crete.

"Don't worry, Icarus," Daedalus said. "This is a difficult problem, but I shall think of a solution."

After days of being locked in the tower, Daedalus and Icarus needed fresh air. Daedalus climbed the stairway and led Icarus to the rooftop of the tower. From there, they watched the gulls and eagles soaring and gliding through the air.

"I have an idea," said Daedalus. "King Minos may rule the land and the sea, but he does not rule the air!"

"But only birds can fly," said Icarus.

"That is because they have wings," said Daedalus. "I want you to help me catch some birds. We need feathers."

Daedalus watched the way birds use their wings to take off and fly. He studied the way feathers fit together to cover a bird's wings. Daedalus laid out rows of feathers. He sewed them together with linen thread and a needle that he carried in his pouch. Finally, Daedalus softened some beeswax until it was sticky. With the wax, Daedalus fastened the rows of feathers together.

At last he was finished. Icarus saw that his father had made two beautiful pairs of wings.

"Son, we have much to learn about flying," Daedalus said. "We will practice many mornings to become strong and skillful enough to fly all the way across the Aegean."

They practiced flying every day. Their muscles became strong, and they increased their skill with their wings.

"Son," Daedalus said one day, "I think we are ready to go. It is important that you heed my words. If you fly too low and too close to the waves, your feathers will get damp. If that happens, your wings will be too heavy to keep you up in the air.

"And if you fly too high," he went on, "the heat of the sun will melt the wax that holds your wings together."

"I understand, Father," said Icarus, but he was barely listening. He was eager to leap into the air again.

As soon as his father finished telling Icarus not to fly too low or too high, the boy ran to the very edge of the rooftop and leaped off. He flapped his outspread wings and headed for the sea with Daedalus close behind him.

The father and son rode the rising currents of air like birds. They made long, slow turns, first one way and then the other in the brilliant blue sky.

But Icarus was becoming reckless. He began diving behind his father when he wasn't watching.

"We are like gods!" Icarus shouted.

Daedalus told his son to stay close behind him.

Icarus beat his wings harder and rose up and up. The warmth of the sun felt good on his back. He rose higher still.

The sun melted the wax on Icarus' wings. Suddenly he dropped straight down, down into the cold sea!

When Daedalus looked back, he could not see his son. Daedalus flew in circles looking for the boy. At last Daedalus flew close enough to the water to see feathers floating on the sea. His beloved son had drowned.

Daedalus wept as he flew home.

Daedalus spent the rest of his days searching the skies for the son who thought he could fly as high as the gods.

Ali Baba

Adapted by Jennifer Boudart
Illustrated by Anthony Lewis

In ancient times, there was a man named Ali Baba. He lived in Persia. Ali Baba was a simple woodcutter.

One day, while Ali Baba was working high in the trees, a group of riders rode beneath his tree. Ali Baba counted them. There were forty riders. It was well known that a band of forty thieves traveled around Persia. They stole anything and everything. They did not mind hurting people to do it.

"Open sesame!" Ali Baba heard their leader say.

A door opened in the rocks. Ali Baba watched the thieves go inside with their heavy bags and come out with nothing.

When the thieves had gone, Ali Baba went before the wall.

"Open sesame!" Ali Baba said, and the door opened again.

The cave was filled with coins, rugs, gold bars, and shiny jewels. Ali Baba grabbed all the riches he could carry.

When Ali Baba's wife saw the riches, she was shocked.

"Did you break the law or hurt anyone?" she asked.

"No," Ali Baba said. He told her about the thieves and their hideout. He told her about the things they had left behind.

Ali Baba used the money to open a shop filled with fine goods at fair prices. It was soon a busy place.

It was a long time before the thieves returned to their hideout. When they did, the thieves discovered that they had been robbed.

"Go to town," the captain said to the smartest thief. "Find a poor man who is newly rich. Get his name. We will get even with him!"

The thief went to town dressed like a trader. The first shop he visited belonged to Ali Baba.

Morgiana, Ali Baba's good friend, was working in the shop.

"I am a trader," the thief said. "I have never seen this shop."

"It is new," Morgiana said. "It is Ali Baba's. It just opened."

The thief smiled and left the shop.

The thief went back to his captain.

"I have a name. It's Ali Baba," the thief said. "He just opened the shop. He lives the life of a rich man."

"Ali Baba will be sorry!" the captain said.

The captain gave his smartest thief a piece of white chalk.

"Return to Ali Baba's shop," the captain said. "Mark an **X** on the door so we will know it. We will break into the shop and teach Ali Baba a lesson."

After dark, the thief returned to the shop. The street was almost empty. He saw only one woman. The thief smiled.

The woman was Morgiana. She remembered that smile.

The thief marked an **X** on Ali Baba's shop.

Morgiana guessed the mark meant trouble for Ali Baba, so she marked an **X** on all the doors along the street.

That night, the thieves did not know which shop to strike. The thieves were angry, but the captain had another plan.

The thieves lined up twenty mules. Each mule carried two large oil barrels. The thieves climbed into the empty barrels.

The captain led the mules to Ali Baba's shop.

"I have come to sell my oil," the captain said. "There is no room at the inn. I wondered if I might sleep in your stable."

"Stables are for mules," Ali Baba said. "Stay in my house."

Ali Baba took the man home with him. The captain took the mules to the stable. He whispered into each barrel.

"Stay here until you hear my whistle," the captain said.

The captain was not Ali Baba's only guest. Morgiana was also staying with Ali Baba's family. Morgiana didn't think the man would mind if she took a bit of oil to heat water for tea. In the stable, as she turned the lid on one of the barrels, a voice whispered, "Is it time?"

"No, not yet," Morgiana whispered back.

Morgiana knew it meant trouble for Ali Baba. She rolled up some hay, set it on fire, then opened the lid of one barrel.

"Go quietly or this fire goes in with you," Morgiana said.

The man jumped out and ran. She went to every barrel and said the same thing. Morgiana scared away all the men.

Morgiana returned to the house where Ali Baba was having dinner with his guest. The guest was wearing a very beautiful robe. Morgiana noticed he kept reaching beneath it. She saw a flash of silver. He was hiding a knife!

"Ali Baba," said Morgiana, "I must dance for your friend."

Morgiana danced with scarves. She circled the man's chair and tied him up.

"This man wants to harm you, Ali Baba," Morgiana said.

Ali Baba's guards took the man to jail.

"Morgiana, you saved my family," Ali Baba said.

Many towns had been robbed by the forty thieves. Each town offered money to anyone who caught them.

Ali Baba knew just what to do with the money. He gave it to Morgiana so she could open her own shop.

"I cannot take it," Morgiana said. "This money would make your life perfect."

"My life is already perfect," Ali Baba said. "I have good friends like you!"

The End